ACTIVE HORMONES

VISHAL KUMAR

Dedicated to the infinite power that strengthens me

And

Dedicated at the feet of the parents who gave the basis of life

Message to the Reader

Lots of love,

This adolescence is like a fair. A fair that everyone wants to enjoy to the fullest. Where everyone wants to get everything available in the fair. Where everyone wants to eat every dish, but after eating some dishes, their stomach gets full but their heart is not satisfied. A fair which everyone enjoys but still some of everyone's desires remain unfulfilled. This story is also about adolescence and unfulfilled desires.

Active Hormones

It was winter afternoon, the sun was dispersing the heat of its rays. In this cold it was doing the work of medicine. The sun's warm rays made life feel. And me and my friends were enjoying the moments. We were sitting in the playground near our house and talking about our future and career.

Do you know that this year the cut off of BPSC is very much?... Aman said.

Bhai, I'm not clearing group "D" here and you talking about BPSC. ... Binay Replied.

"Binay, why do always think wrong?... Aman Replied.

"What do you mean?... Binay, asked.

"I was just saying that day by day the competition exams are getting tough. ...Aman said.

Hey guys stop arguing. ...I said

I'm not arguing, please tell him. ...Binay said.

Drop it and look there" one of the active Hormone. ...Aman said

let's take his class.... I said

Hey, Avinav come here Vishal bhaiya is calling you. ...Aman said

A 14 year old boy who is four years away to complete his 18, and to be upto the ground in the pursuit of learning a bike, great it's called real teenager.

Yes Vishal bhaiya, what happened. ...Avinav asked

Nothing has happened but is about to happen.
...I replied

what?... Avinav asked

Your father is going to have a grandson.
...Binay said

Hehehe, why are you kidding. ...Avinav said

Look how is this shameless laughing. ....Aman
said

I don't understand what you are saying.
...Avinav said

Don't you know what's going on, so tell me
where were you last evening. ...I asked

I went to my coaching classes. ...Avinav said

And what is the timing of your coaching
classes? ... I asked

Five o'clock. ... Avinav replied

Then tell me what you were doing around
5o'clock near the chaat stall ? ... I asked

It was a class holiday. ... Avinav replied

Are you talking about M.Kumar Sir's classes? ...
I asked

Yes ... Avinav replied

Do you think all of us are stupid? ... I asked

M.kumar sir's classes are running regularly. ...
Aman said

Sorry Vishal Bhaiya actually I went to my
friend's house. ... Avinav said

Means you bunked your class. ... Aman said

Classes are bunked but he is still lying. ... I said

No, Vishal Bhaiya. ... Avinav replied

You were eating chaat with your girlfriend and
you say that you went to a friend's house. ... I
said

No Vishal Bhaiya it is not what you are
thinking. ... Avinav said

I'm thinking right, now tell me all the truth. ... I
said

Ok Bhaiya but don't you tell my father. ...
Avinav said

Ok. ... I replied

Her name is Riya, I like her but she's not my girlfriend. ... Avinav said

Means you are in his entanglement, are you not? ... Aman asked

Hehehe...Yes Aman Bhaiya. Avinav said

Do you think you will impress her? ... I asked

I don't know but I don't want to lose her. ... Avinav said

Great,"Majnu ki aulad" ... Aman said smiling

Is it necessary to bunk classes in order to impress the girl? ... I asked

Sorry Bhaiya, what should I do? ... Avinav asked

After classes you just give her a little time, If you give her more time than she needs, she

Will never give you value. ... I said

Ok Bhaiya I won't bunk class now. ... Avinav said

Vishal, are you taking his class or helping him.
... Binay said

The child is now grown up, Vishal is giving it a
guideline. ... Aman said

You guys have no other work, you are spoiling
the child. ... Binay said

You don't have a girlfriend, At least let this
child be have a girlfriend. ... Aman said

Saala chutiya ,you will not improve. ... Binay
said

All right now keep your mouth shut. ... Aman
said

Avinav I think you should leave now, here
there is a fight between two donkeys. ... I said

Hehehe...Ok Bhaiya. ... Avinav said

See how Avinav is riding the bike in perfect
Chhapariya style. ... Aman said

Because he is an "Active Hormone" HaHaHa. ...
I said

You all must be thinking that what is this active
hormones? Afterall, why were we all calling

him an active hormone to a boy? What is the reason behind it? Is it a member of any group

whose name is Active Hormones.

Actually not a member of any small group, they are members of a very large group,

about which their members themselves don't. Actually these people are strange

creatures of an amazing category around the world. Usually these creatures are seen roaming on the streets and alleys. Some experts believe that these creatures do not wander, in fact they are engaged in the process of going and coming to school and coaching classes. some experts also believe that some creature score can also be seen near the chaat and momo's stall. Especially at the time when they have bunked their class or is with any of his opposite gender friend. Unfortunately some creature in this category are not able to get education, but mostly are students. Although, some of these creatures are good students, but most of them are son of Majnu. Whom we usually call "Majnu ki aulad" .

There is also some females in these categories. Who calls her self Papa'sangels, Who is

Known in the society as "Papakipari".

These angels have two special hobbies. Firstfly without any wings and second make fly

any one with their own scooty. These angels are very master in riding scooty. Sometimes

these angels turn right by giving a left indicator. Well that's all the things that make them

special. And because of their merits they think they are very special. What is special about

them is their identity in the society. These people are easily recognized because of their age.

Generally these are found at the age of 13 to 19 years. That's why they are known as

teenagers in the society. But they are also known by other names just like minor, youngster,

juvenile, stripling and sweet-sixteen. Many physical and mental changes happen in youngster at this stage of age. These changes are caused by estrogen, progesterone, and testosterone hormones. These are very high active hormones at this age. That's why we all call them as active hormones.

It was Monday morning, Ravi came to my house and called me.I called him inside the house.

what's the matter, this morning at my house? ... I asked

Badi Maa is calling you. ... Ravi said

Is there any work? ... I asked

Exams are coming soon, have to do some studies. ... Ravi Said

Hahaha ...got it. ... I said

Hehehe ...But you have to help in practical also. ... Ravi said

Beta ,do some work by yourself. ... I said

Vishal Bhaiya, please... Ravi said

let's go away from here. ... I said

Ravi came out of the house and said that you have to help in practical any how and ran away by laughing.

After an hour I went to Ravi's house, Ravi was sitting in his courtyard playing a game on his

Mobile and his elder mother (Badi-Maa) was chopping vegetables. Ravi's father Upendra

Singh and elder father (Bade-Bauji) Gajendra Singh had separated but still both had the same courtyar. And this was a good thing, even after being separated, they used to celebrate festivals together in the same courtyard.

Pranaam chachi. … I said

Anita Devi (Ravi's Badi-Maa) –"Jug Jug Jiyo" Beta.

You called me? … I asked

Haan Beta, Khushbu and Ravi's exams are coming soon.

You have to teach them . … Anita Devi said

Ok Chachi, don't worry. … I said

Bahu, look Vishal Bhaiya has come, bring tea for him. … Anita Devi said

After some time Khushbu brought tea. 19 year old girl wearing a white saree as if all the colours of her life have become colour less. It is not an easy thing to become a widow at such a young age, to be robbed of all the desires, to get caught in the quagmire of the evils of the society. I don't know how she hides her pain and suffering behind her smile. But it was hard for me to see her in this condition. Afterall she considered me as her elder brother. Which brother can see his sister in this condition. It is a year old thing when 18 year old flirtatious girl came to this house as a bride. Khushbu was married to Karan Singh, my best friend and the only child of Gajendra Singh. Karan was the youngest job seeker of his locality, he joined BSF in 21 years. After one years of training and two year of posting, at the age of 24 had to marry an 18 year old girl due to family pressure. But Karan knew about the situation at the border, that's why he first got Khushbu's admission in 11th class. Karan wanted that the Khushbu should become so capable that he would never have to rely on any one else. Khushbu was very happy to marry Karan. And the none day it happened what we all feared, the situation at the border was not good, Karan had got a call from there. It was not yet 18 days for marriage that Karan had to go for his duty. Four days later the news came that eight soldiers of the BSF were martyred, one of them was the name of Karan Singh. The next day the military truck brought Karan's dead body to the home. Whenever my friend came home, Iused to greet him with a great hug. And today I had to give the last fare well to the same friend on my shoulder. This time was very difficult for Karan's family. The color of the mehndi of the bride's hands had not even come off and the winds of time snatched her husband from her. Who can stop those who have gone, but the mountain of trouble falls on those who have to live by their memories. Apart from the memories of Karan, if Khushbu has anything left, it is sorrow, pain, tears and white Saree. But there was a light of hope that Karan had lit, that is Khushbu's education which can change her fate. I am glad that I got a chance to help Khushbu and make my friend's dream come true.

***

It was evening, we were all sitting at our haunt, This playground was our only haunt where we used to live life with friends for a moment away from the responsibilities of our life. Where we used to share our joys and sorrows, we used to talk about our unfulfilled wishes and dreams. By the way, our group was of only three people, which was Me, Aman and Binay. But the specialty of this place was that during the evening, someone or the other used to join our group. Whether it is children, young or old. Those people loved to enjoy our company. We were all talking, suddenly Avinav came running after seeing us.

Vishal bhaiya you are genius..... Avinav said.

What did your" Vishal bhaiya" do? Aman asked.

Vishal bhaiya your idea worked. Avinav said.

Why, "What happened".....? I asked.

I was doing the same as you said, was coming straight home from coaching without talking to Riya. And Riya used to wait for me everyday near the chaat stall and

finally she interrupted me yesterday. Avinav said.

So what did she say....? Aman asked.

She said.... "Hi Avinav, how are you....?" then i just said fine and started ignoring her, Then she asked me.... are you busy now a days? Avinav said excitedly.

What happened after that....? Aman asked.

Then I said yes there is some work at my home..... and I walked away from there. Avinav said.

Aman - Well played, you did well to get out
from there. Aman said.

What do you mean? Avinav asked.

Oh duffer, If you had talked to her at that time,
she would have become normal again. I said.

Then it's so good that I didn't say anything and
I walked away from there. Avinav said.

Why....did you want to talk to her. Aman asked
while pulling Avinav's leg.

Yes but I wasn't able to talk at that time.
Avinav said.

Why so......? Aman asked.

My condition was getting worse, my hands and
feet were trembling, I could not understand
what to do, so I had to leave from there.
Avinav said.

Got it....... I said.

Avinav - What do you understand "Vishal
bhaiya"? Avinav asked in confusion.

It's just that your heartbeat started
accelerating....... you wanted to say a lot,
but.... there was silence on your mouth, your

heart and your mind wouldn't know anything...... you must have lost your senses. The whole body would be trembling from head to toe........... yet this situation would be making you feel a unique happiness. so you didn't understand what to do and ran away from her. I said.

Avinav - How do you know ! Avinav asked surprisingly.

Because, it's a kind of disease. I said jokingly.

Avinav - What kind of disease is this, are there any signs of weakness? Avinav asked seriously.

No it's a very dangerous disease. I said while pulling Avinav's leg.

Avinav - Why are you scaring me, just tell me the name of this disease. Avinav asked fearfully.

Bhai , you are suffering from " Prem Rog "......... Aman said laughlingly.

Hehehe...it's not true. Avinav said by blushing.

I can understand why you are blushing. I said smilingly.

Look there...... Mayank got busy on his phone again , after all...... to whom he talks so much. Aman said.

Mayank the most unique active hormone in our locality, When no one is visible at 5 o'clock in the morning, then Mayank is seen, He is visible even when everyone is doing morning walk at 6 in the morning. , even after school at 2:30 o'clock in the afternoon, everyone goes to their home, even then he is seen only in this playground. The special thing is that whenever Mayank is seen, he seems to be busy on the phone.

'Must be talking to his girlfriend.' Avinav said.

'I can see, but... who is his girlfriend.' Aman asked.

"What to tell 'Aman bhaiya'..... She is the most beautiful and attractive girl in our school.....all the boys go crazy after her, none of the senior boys in our school could impress her, and even if she was impressed by her junior." Avinav replied.

'What do you mean mayank is junior to his girlfriend?' Aman asked.

'Yes she is in 12th standard' Avinav replied.

"Great" But how did Mayank do this miracle? Aman asked by laughing.

'There is also an interesting story behind it...Last year there was an inter house cricket competition in our school. The final match was between Dayanand House and Vivekananda House. Kaamna was cheering up her "Dayanand House" And there was a deep silence in the whole Vivekananda House,.......there was no hope of victory in sight. 6 batsmen were out, our captain Manjeet Bhaiya was also out in 15 runs. Mayank Yadav, Vivekananda House's last hope and vice-captain, still stood on the field with strong determination and in front was the fastest bowler of our school, Ajmal Hussain of 12th standard. Nine runs were needed to win in just two balls. Mayank took off his helmet and looked at Manjeet Bhaiya taking his position on strike. Fifth ball of the last over and the bowler hits a brilliant bounce and Mayank took four runs playing the upper cut just like Sehwag. For a moment there was a smile among the students of Vivekananda House and again there was silence in the whole house, even in Dayanand House. Last ball of the last over and a brilliant yorker effort by the bowler and just like MS Dhoni, Mayank sent the ball outside the boundary line while hitting the helicopter shot.

What happened after that...? Aman asked.

'What was to happen then.......Dayanand House lost the match and Kaamna lost her heart' Avinav replied.

'It's good, Mayank got some advantage of playing cricket.' I said.

'This is nothing, Mayank has had s*x eight times so far.' Avinav replied in excitement.

"Beta" learn something from Mayank. Aman said jokingly.

Hehehe...Aman bhaiya, I'm trying... Avinav replied by blushing.

***

Sunday morning off, a holiday that sometimes becomes a necessary working day. Like bringing ration, cleaning the house or getting the bike serviced. And I went out with my Activa 3G for servicing, It was a different matter that the whole world was using 4G, whether it was Jio's free service or the Activa 4G scooty. And i was carrying Activa 3G along with my responsibilities. Yes but one thing is that my responsibility and my scooty never left me alone. And the service of such a friend is also necessary, now when servicing has to be done then it should be done by an expert. Just like our 'Kareem bhai'. Kareem bhai is world famous in our area, hey don't take me as a joke. The difference is that Kareem Bhai's garage is not a five star garage. But no less than a five star garage. Yes, it is different that during servicing you will not be made to sit on the sofa in the waiting room, but as soon as you go, you will be given seats made of old tires to sit on. Don't know about the air condition, but as soon as you sit, the stand fan will be turned towards you. And as soon as you sit, you will be served "kulhad chai" from the tea stall next to the Shiva temple. Now tell me, will such service be available in any five star garage? And as far as the servicing of the scooty is concerned, Kareem Bhai says that his grandfather used to service the Nawabs of Lucknow from horse shoe to royal chariot and expensive cars. Don't know about his grandfather, but when Kareem Bhai speaks, then "Lakhnawi Andaaz" drips from his mouth instead of paan. Yes kareem bhai is overstated person but he is a very experienced mechanic.

Salaam Vishal Bhaiya...Kabir said.

Salaam Kabir.... where is Kareem Bhai ? I asked.

He has gone to the market. Kabir replied.

Have they gone to the market or the paan shop? I laughed and asked.

Hahaha...Vishal Bhaiya , you are too much. Kabir replied.

Ok... tell me how is your mother's health? I asked.

There is no significant improvement and the medicine is also increasing. Kabir replied.

Doctor has prescribed any checkup etc. I asked.

Yes checkup has been done but no report has come yet. Kabir replied.

"Oh" and how is your study? I asked.

Study is going well but had to leave tuition. Kabir replied.

"Kabir" I can understand, I have told you many times that come to me, I will teach you. I said.

But Vishal Bhaiya, I will not be able to pay the fees. Kabir replied.

I have ever asked you for a fee? I asked.

No... Vishal Bhaiya. Kabir replied.

Then don't think too much, come if you get time. I said.

Ok Bhaiya , but now tell me what is the problem with the scooty. Kabir asked.

There is no problem, just need to be serviced. I said.

You sit down we do it right away. Kabir said.

I sat on the seat of the tire and watched Kabir at work. Looking at Kabir, it is known that maturity comes from circumstances, not from age. Although Kabir is also one of those active hormones. But this hormone is very different from other hormones. 15 year old Kabir Ansari is passing through the same phase of age at which all the active hormones are passing through, but still he is aware of his responsibilities. But this boy is amazing, he does bury himself in the garage during the day and books at night. The heart becomes happy seeing the spirit of Kabir. But sometimes Kabir gets a little confused, although it is natural to behave like this at this age. One thing is sure, the one who fought with this stage of age has won half the battle of life. And Kabir's flag of victory was yet to be hoisted.

***

Once upon a time I was teaching social reform movement to Khushbu and Ravi.

Ishwar Chandra Vidyasagar took up the challenge and got the first widow remarriage done on his own on 7 December 1856 in Kolkata. He prepared a public opinion for widow remarriage. Due to his efforts, the Widow-Remarriage Act was passed in the year 1856. He married his only son to a widow.

Vishal Bhaiya do you think even after so many years of independence women have got their rightful rights? Khushbu asked with a painful fake smile.

To tell the truth, the struggle of human with human and women with society has been going on for ages. That's why whether reforms come or not in the society, but you got to keep struggling and fight for your dreams. I said to Khushbu.

You are talking about fighting for dreams but... I don't think a widow has the right to dream in this society. Khushbu said.

Why do you think so? I asked.

Because I can't remember the last time I dreamed, You tell me, do you see even a single dream alive in the eyes of this widow. Khushbu replied.

Look, everyone in the world has the right to dream because everything in the world can be taken away from you but it is your dream that no one can take away from you. So keep dreaming because it is the dreams that make you feel alive. I said.

What should I do, I can't fulfill my dreams even if I want to. Khushbu replied.

So fulfill the dream of the one who dreamed for you. I said.

Khushbu could not say anything, her eyes became moist and she started looking towards Ravi. I thought Khushbu should be given some time, I asked both of them to revise the chapter and left from there.

It was evening time and our haunt was missing us. So we also went to our haunt. Went there and saw today's view was different, Avinav was already sitting there laughing with his friends. On seeing us, Avinav started laughing hysterically.

What happened Bhai, why are you laughing so much. Aman asked.

Aman Bhaiya, amazing incident happened. Avinav replied.

What has become so amazing? Binay asked.

Actually this afternoon Sonu was watching po*n by closing the door of his room. He closed the door and forgot to close the window, Unaware of his fun, Sonu did not notice that his father was watching him for the last 5 minutes through the window... With all the fun, as soon as Sonu put his hand inside his pant, a sound was heard "Beta Sonu,.......what is going on.....?". Avinav said while having fun.

Then what happened to Sonu....? Aman asked.

His father beat him with a belt and also took away his mobile. Avinav replied.

And also tell that Sonu's father has told him to stop hanging out with "Chutiya Avinav" from today. Rohit said laughlingly.

Saala Baklol......was it necessary to say this? Avinav said angrily.

Hey Avinav, why are you getting so angry, Rohit is telling the truth, you are the biggest

"Bhakchonhar" of this locality. Aman said with laughing.

Poor Avinav was laughing a while back and has now become a laughing stock himself. Still plucking up courage, he took a brazen laugh and asked "Aman Bhaiya, has this ever happened to you....?".

Not with me but happened to a friend of mine. Aman replied.

With whom did it happen and what was the incident? Avinav asked in great excitement.

Look at this worthless boy, asking how excitedly. Binay said.

Vishal, do you remember the incident that happened with Kundan? Aman asked.

How could I forget the that incident, Neither was that incident worth forgetting, nor was Kundan. Kundan was an amazing character, very thin, looking at which anyone could say that he would definitely be an international player of Ludo. Whenever there was any tension, depression or problem, he used to become stress free by playing Ludo. By the way,.....you must be understanding the meaning of playing Ludo, Shaking...... Shaking........ and only Shaking...... He was big hearted, he used to spread happiness among people. Especially those people who were afraid to buy po*n cassettes in the market. There were not only youths in the group of those people, some uncles and old people were also involved. Kundan was a cassettes shop on wheels for those, All kinds of movie cassettes were available with him, Desi-Videshi, Tarzan ,Lady-Tarzan, Indian-Kamasutra, Chinese-Kamasutra. Everything was free, he never asked anyone for money. It was different that he used to get the treat of Chaat, Samosa and Lachha Paratha everyday.

Yes... I remember. I said.

Looks like something funny happened, now tell me too Aman Bhaiya. Avinav said.

It is a matter of time when there were neither smartphones nor computers in every house. People used to rent DVDs to watch movies, only a few people had DVDs and amplifier systems. At that time it was not so easy to watch po*n as it is today. Had to find a right place and means, That's why Kundan used to make all our arrangements for us. And that day also all the arrangements were done at Kundan's house. Aman said.

What happened then Aman Bhaiya....? Avinav asked in excitement.

It was afternoon, Kundan's father had gone on duty and there was no one at home, all the people had gone to village. Kundan had his own DVD and amplifier system at home. We all reached Kundan's house to watch the movie. Kundan inserted the cassette and started the movie. Gradually, someone started rubbing the pillow, so someone's tower started giving signal and someone started trying to control their emotions. Seeing all this Vishal said to Kundan"sirf hilayega hi, ya kuch khilayega bhi?". Hearing this, Kundan laughed like a shameless person and went to the kitchen to make Maggi. then suddenly the electricity went out. Due to electricity our whole plan got flopped and it started getting hot, so we all came out and sat under the tree in the courtyard. By then Maggi was ready, Kundan brought Maggi and we all ate and then returned to our homes. Aman said whole the story.

Hey Aman Bhaiya.....where did any incident happen? Avinav asked.

The real incident was about to happen, we all had returned to our house but Kundan slept on the cot under the same tree and did not know when it was 4:00 in the evening. Kundan's father had returned and as usual he was about to take a bath. He often used to do any work while listening to the songs of Mohammed Rafi. He turned on the amplifier and then turned up the volume but the song was not playing, then he saw that the DVD was switched off. As soon as he switched on the whole house started humming with the sound of "oh yeah oh yeah do it faster, just make me your bit*h, take me so high...F-Fu*k...mmmhh.." Hearing the sound, Kundan woke up and while trying to escape, slipped and broke his leg. Even though the leg was broken, the father also beat him separately. Poor Kundan kept walking around with a plaster on his leg for two months. Aman told the whole incident.

Hahaha...It was a very funny incident, but where is Kundan Bhaiya now? Avinav asked.

He is currently working in some garment factory in Delhi. Aman replied.

Kundan now hates Maggi. I said.

But why so? Avinav asked.

It has actually stuck cassettes in DVD several times before due to power outages. At that time, Kundan used to open the cover of the DVD with a screw driver and take out the cassette. But he forgot to take out the cassette in the process of making and eating Maggi on that day. But I think, I was the reason Kundan was caught, not Maggi. I said by laughing.

Now I have to stay away from you too. Avinav said by laughing.

Some things bring back old memories. We laugh at the antics of these active hormones, but forget that we too used to be active hormones. It is true that "Adolescence is that narrow street of life that everyone has to pass through one day or the other." I walked towards my house smiling remembering old things. As soon as I reached home, I saw a scene which I absolutely disliked in this society. I saw that outside my house my grandmother is sitting on the chair and next to her 'Phulwa Chachi' is sitting on the ground. That's because Phulwa Chachi was from Musahar caste. I hate this caste system, I don't know when and who created this caste system, it is sad that even after so many years of independence, there is no significant change in the thinking of the people. What would have gone wrong if my grandmother had given a chair to Phulwa Chachi to sit? Perhaps Phulwa Chachi's fault was that she was born in a Musahar caste.

The Musahar caste originated at a time when there was a terrible famine in northern parts of India and Bihar. To calm the fire of their hunger, some community people started eating rats, then they are known as Musahar till date. The word Musahar in Hindi means rats and diet, people who eat rats. Although this statement is bitter but true that we all are living in a hypocritical society. There is a proverb in English that the strongest man survives. Living in such a bad condition by eating rats is an example of such a thing. Despite this, many people look at these people with inferiority complex.

What happened 'Phulwa Chachi'? I asked.

'Beta' all my efforts are ruined, Shiksha has left her college and came back home and started saying that she would drop out of college. Phulwa Chachi said by crying.

Why did she do that? I asked.

Don't know, just says that she was very unlucky to be born from my womb. Phulwa Chachi said.

"Oh"..... Chachi, don't cry. I will talk to her.

Beta, go home now and explain to her, I am getting very discomfort, I don't understand anything, what should I do? Phulwa Chachi said.

When I went to Shiksha's house, I saw that Shiksha was sitting sadly on the floor leaning against the wall. Even if the poor girl could sit, where would she sit? It was a small one-room house with old walls and an asbestos roof. I just asked, how are you, Shiksha, when did you come from college?

Who cares what I am like, and mom must have told you that I am leaving college, Nothing can be digested in mother's stomach, she keeps on spoiling me with everything. Shiksha vented out her anger and said.

Yes you are absolutely right no one cares how you are, except your mother. Well, tell me what problem happened to you due to which you are leaving college. I asked.

I don't have any problem, I just don't feel like going to college now. Shiksha replied.

This is not an answer... Look, if you keep running away from your problems in life like this, you will never be able to solve your problems. Now you tell me whether you will share your problems with your Vishal Bhaiya or not. I said.

I'm suffocating in that place Vishal Bhaiya. I don't dare stay there for a moment. Shiksha replied.

But why so...? I asked.

No one treats me well there. There was a senior who used to talk to me but now she too is gone. My roommate also talks to her boyfriend on the phone all day long. She talks to me only in times of need, I even wrote to her practically several times but still she doesn't treat me well. Shiksha replied.

This is wrong but why are they behaving like this? I asked.

Because in the whole college I am the only one who uses a keypad phone and everyone else has a smartphone. Neither do I have good clothes nor dressing sense, I have not studied in English medium school nor do I know how to maintain the status of those people. The people who came from government school like me are the same people who changed themselves after joining college. Only I am the one who did not change myself because I did not have money. that's why they look down on me and make fun of me. Shiksha said with wet eyes.

Just that and you are ready to leave college. I asked.

This may be a small thing for you, but even after studying so hard, forget being attracted to me, no one even wants to be friends with me. Leave aside girls, not even any boy wants to be my friend. Sometimes I feel jealous seeing girls who keep talking to their boyfriends all day long. Shiksha replied like an innocent girl.

Okay, I understand, you tell me, do you want to have a friend or a boyfriend? I asked jokingly.

Damn it Bhaiya, I just want to make a good friend who understands and supports me. Shiksha said shyly and smilingly.

It felt good to have a smile on your face. Don't you want to have a similar smile on your mother's face? Just look at your mother once. This is the 'Devi' who is teaching you by washing utensils in people's homes. And you are insulting the womb of this Devi from whom you were born. Have you ever wondered why an uneducated woman named her daughter Shiksha ?...Have you ever wondered why the one who herself was deprived of knowledge is making so much effort to make you knowledgeable?...now tell me do you have any answer? I asked.

Sorry Vishal Bhaiya... Shiksha replied.

What does sorry mean, do you have the answer or not. I asked.

No...Shiksha replied.

So search for answers and till then do what your mother wants from you. Fulfill your mother's dream by completing your studies. Become something and prove to the world that a person is greater not by his caste but by his thoughts and actions. I said.

As soon as Shiksha heard my words, she fell at her mother's feet and started crying bitterly.

Maa...... I promise you that I will not ask for anything from you, just keep your blessings on me and never leave me alone....Shiksha said by crying.

Pagli, my blessings are always with you. Phulwa Chachi said emotionally.

It's surprising that it's been so long since I came here, yet no one has asked me for a cup of tea. I said it jokingly.

Have a sit Vishal Bhaiya , I will bring it. Shiksha spoke with tears in her eyes and a smile on her lips.

After some time Shiksha comes with tea...

Tea is a very well-prepared , But tell me one thing, how do you make such good tea? I asked.

What about tea?... The better we boil the tea leaves, the better the tea will be. Shiksha replied.

Exactly right, just as tea leaves have to be boiled to make good tea, similarly we too have to struggle to make a good life. I said.

Vishal Bhaiya , you are right, but sometimes I get confused. Shiksha replied.

It's natural to be confused, but don't consider yourself weak....Well, you must have read the law of gravitation. The theory states that every object in the world attracts every other object. I said.

Yes. Shiksha replied.

Then why do you feel that you will not be able to attract anyone in this world?...That's because you consider yourself weak. And maybe you are also right because the object in the world whose attractive force is more than other objects, attracts the other object. So if you want to get people's attention, you have to become great. I said.

If I didn't become great?...Shiksha asked.

So be a small but important part of something great. I replied.

Shiksha is one of our active hormones which has more complaints than desires. It is natural to have desires at this age, but if the desires are not fulfilled then those desires turn into complaints. And Shiksha is going through the same situation , After passing her board exams, it was very challenging for Shiksha to clear the Jharkhand Combine Entrance Exam and get into a good polytechnic college. And even after so much effort, if the circumstances is not favourable then it feels bad.

***

The exams were over and that day came for which not only the students but also children, old and young all were waiting. Of course, whenever we talk about UP, Bihar and Jharkhand and there is no mention of Holi, then this story seems incomplete. It was Holi and Ravi was fully prepared. The staircase leading to the terrace attached to the wall passed through the courtyard itself. Ravi was hiding under the stairs with gulaal in his hands. Khushbu was going towards the terrace when suddenly Ravi held her hand from behind and pulled her towards him.

Leave my hand, anyone will see. Khushbu said scaredly.

There is no one at home except you and me. Ravi replied.

let me go, I have a lot of work. Khushbu released her hand and said.

Ravi held Khushbu's waist with one hand and pulled her towards him and applied gulal on Khushbu's cheeks with the other hand. Khushbu started looking lovingly into Ravi's eyes. Both lost in each other's eyes. Ravi brought his lips in front of Khushbu's lips, Khushbu's heartbeats and breathing started increasing. Ravi started feeling Khushbu's increasing breathing. Khushbu closed her eyes and Ravi was about to kiss her when suddenly there was a sound.

Ravi what are you doing, she is your bhabi. Anita Devi said.

As soon as Anita Devi came, she slapped Ravi hard on his cheek.

Besharam, how dare you do all this? Have you even forgotten that she is your elder brother's widow? Anita Devi said.

As soon as Ravi was slapped, he bowed down completely and did not utter a word from his mouth. And after that Anita Devi's anger knew no bounds, she pulled Khushbu's hair and started beating her.

Kameenee...kulta...firstly, you swallowed my son while coming and then you feel like having fun with your own brother-in-law. Anita Devi said.

While beating Khushbu, Anita Devi started crying and sat there and held her head.

Hey Bhagwan, I kept her safe from the whole world but I didn't know that a thief is sitting right in my house. Anita Devi said.

Anita Devi was a very soft hearted woman and she knew that if her husband came to know about the entire incident then he would stop Khushbu from studying and there would be fights in the family. Therefore, Anita Devi made both of them understand that this should not happen again and hushed up the whole matter.

***

It was 10 in the morning, Kareem Bhai's garage used to open by this time. When I reached the garage I saw that it was closed today. When I asked the shopkeeper next door, I came to know that Kareem Bhai had gone to someone's funeral. I came back home. Around 1 o'clock in the afternoon someone knocked at the door, I opened the door and saw Kabir standing there and there was dusty soil on his kurta. As soon as he saw me, he hugged me and started crying.

Vishal Bhaiya, I lost everything now there's nothing left. Kabir said.

Hey don't cry tell me what happened. I asked.

Ammi became dear to God, She left me alone in this cruel world. Kabir said by crying.

I made him sit on a chair and gave him water to drink. He drank water while crying.

Calm down Kabir, I can understand your pain. But we human beings are helpless and can't do anything. This is the rule of the world. Whoever has come into this world will have to go one day.... Be strong Kabir and don't forget that your Ammi's blessings are with you. I said.

When Ammi is no more, then how will Ammi's blessings remain? Kabir said.

Don't say this Kabir, blessings have a lot of power especially when those prayers are from your mother. I said.

Does this really happen? Kabir asked.

Yes Kabir, Mother's blessings can change even a broken destiny. I said.

After my Ammi left, my destiny has also died. Kabir said.

Don't hurt your mother's soul by saying this. Wherever she is at this moment, she too must be feeling pain after seeing you in this condition. She has left this selfish world and gone to God. Farewell her with love. I said.

Yes, she was suffering a lot in this world and I couldn't even do anything for her. Kabir said.

So now you can do what your Ammi wanted. I said.

My poor Ammi was very simple, she never wanted anything from me. Kabir said.

Your mother named you, right? I asked.

Yes... Kabir replied.

Do you know what Kabir means? I asked.

No...Kabir replied.

Kabir means " The Great"...In fact it is one of the many names of Allah. Allah calls Himself Al-Kabeer in the Quran. I said.

Does Allah have many other names? Kabir asked innocently, fighting back his tears.

There is no end to the names of God... Kabir, But people call God by different names. I replied.

It means I am named after "Allah". Kabir said.

Yes and it also means that your Ammi wanted you to be as "Great" as your name. I replied.

You are right Vishal bhaiya, I have to fulfill my Ammi's unfulfilled wishes. Kabir said.

After some time, I left on my scooter to take Kabir to his home. As soon as we reached near the Bada Masjid of Ramzanpur, Kabir said that he should be dropped here. I dropped him there. That day I was seeing Kabir for the last time. Later someone told that Kabir has gone to his khala's (aunt's) house in Hazaribagh forever.

***

It was 4:00 in the evening. My mother's anger was sky high.

I have been telling your father since morning that all the green vegetables in the house are finished but he doesn't understand anything. Maa said angrily.

When I did not reply, mother again became very angry.

Both father and son are alike, Let them ask for food at night, I will give salt and roti to both of them to eat. Maa said.

Before my mother's anger could increase further, I picked up my wallet and set out for the market. While passing through the playground, I saw that our group was sitting there. Seeing them all sitting, I turned my scooty towards them.

Look Vishal bhaiya has come, now your work will be done. Pointing to Mayank, Avinav said.

Oh yes, Vishal bhaiya can you help me a little? Mayank asked.

What kind of help? I asked.

Actually, I needed some money. Mayank replied.

How much? I asked.

Only 2000 rupees. Avinav said laughingly.

Bhai, we all needed only 2 rupees to buy a kite in school days. Which airplane will you buy for 2000 rupees? I asked.

Vishal bhaiya, he is not going to tell you anything. Let me tell you, he actually needs money for his girlfriend's birthday celebration. Avinav said with full enjoyment.

Need 2000 rupees just to celebrate birthday? I asked.

Not only this, he has also taken thousand rupees from Aman Bhaiya. Avinav said while mocking Mayank.

Waah Beta, What gift will you give her worth the full 3000 rupees? I asked.

The entire market and what else. Avinav again made fun of Mayank and said.

Don't be too smart otherwise you will be beaten right now. Mayank scolded Avinav.

Mayank, leave Avinav and tell me how you will return the 3000 rupees you are borrowing. Aman asked.

There are four buffaloes in his stable, If he mix one liter of water in 4 liters of milk every day, then he will return your money within two days. Avinav said laughingly.

Everyone started laughing after hearing Abhinav's words, except Mayank.

Vishal bhaiya, tell Avinav to keep quiet otherwise a murder will be committed by my hands. Mayank said angrily.

Calm down Mayank, if you commit murder and go to jail then who will take care of your buffaloes, who will bathe them, feed them fodder and who milk them twice a day? I replied.

After listening to me, this time again everyone started laughing, even Mayank too.

Everyone was laughing when suddenly I remembered that if I did not go home with vegetables today, So instead of eating at dinner i will get scolded. So without wasting any time I immediately left from there towards the market.

Well a question is coming to my mind. Avinav said.

Regarding Mayank? Aman asked.

No, Regarding Vishal bhaiya. Avinav replied.

Now what are you thinking about Vishal Bhaiya? Mayank asked.

Just about Vishal Bhaiya's girlfriend. Avinav replied.

He doesn't have a girlfriend. Mayank replied.

You and I know this, whether he ever had a girlfriend or not, only Aman Bhaiya can tell us. Avinav said.

Yes, Avinav is right about this, please tell us Aman Bhaiya, did Vishal bhaiya ever have a girlfriend or not? Mayank asked.

Aman looked at Binay, Binay's eyes seemed to say that there was no need for him to answer the questions of stupid hormones.

During our high school days, Vishal used to make fun of people who were in love. But he had no idea that one day he himself would be entangled in a love affair. Aman said ignoring Binay.

Means, Vishal bhaiya also has a love story. Please Aman bhaiya, tell us his story too. Avinav said.

It was the first day of "Argha" of Chhath festival. Vishal was lighting diya on the banks of the "Chhath ghat". Then suddenly a gust of wind came and the diya Vishal was lighting was about to be extinguished when suddenly someone covered it with both his hands. Vishal couldn't help but look at her soft and beautiful hand like of lotus. As soon as Vishal raised his head to look at her, Vishal's eyes met hers and for a moment, Vishal got lost in her beautiful eyes. Vishal, who was intoxicated with her beauty, did not even realize that the matchstick burning in his hand was completely burnt and as soon as the flame left Vishal's fingers, Vishal regained consciousness. Vishal throws away the burnt matchstick and takes his burnt fingers in his mouth. Seeing this action of Vishal, she starts laughing loudly and hearing his voice, Vishal's heart starts beating faster because the more She was beautiful, her voice was more beautiful. Aman told how love started.

It was really quite romantic. Mayank said.

Yes, but what was the girl's name? Avinav asked excitedly.

Her name was Jenny. She was Vishal's cousin Roshni's classmate. They both studied in Carmel School. Roshni had invited Jenny to the festival. Aman replied.

Then Roshni didi must have helped Vishal bhaiya a lot. Mayank asked smilingly.

Yes, she was Roshni who had told Vishal that Jenny also liked him very much but she was waiting for the right moment. Aman replied.

Then what happened after that? Avinav asked.

Like every true love story, this love story also ended the same way. two lovers separated forever. Aman said sadly.

But why did this happen? Avinav asked sadly.

Because Jenny had gone far away from Vishal forever, so far from where no one has ever returned. Aman controlled his emotions and replied.

***

At last the day had come for which Mayank was eagerly waiting, after all Mayank had borrowed money for this very day. Mayank was waiting for Kaamna at Fushbangla Chowk. After some time, Kaamna reached there on her scooter.

Happy Birthday my dear. Mayank said.

Thankyou. Kaamna replied.

You sit in the back seat, now I will drive. Mayank said.

As you wish my lord. Kaamna replied smilingly.

After some time, both of them reached a hotel. Mayank had already booked a room. Kaamna came to know about this after visiting there.

What is your intention Mayank? Kaamna asked in a very soft voice while smiling.

First come with me then ask something later. Mayank said.

As soon as Kaamna opened the door, she was surprised to see the view inside. The whole room was decorated with red and white balloons and there were many candles all around the room. The whole room was smelling of lavender. There was a very beautiful red velvet cake placed on a tea table in the middle of the room. Next to the cake was a Champagne bottle immersed in a small bucket filled with ice. There was a pair of wine glasses nearby. A white bedsheet was spread on the bed on which a huge heart was made from rose petals and in the middle of the heart was written "LOVE YOU" with rose petals.

Happy Birthday to you...Happy Birthday to you...Happy Birthday dear Kaamna...Happy Birthday to you. Mayank wished her.

It's so romantic dear, thank you so much. Kaamna said while hugging Mayank.

Mayank closed the door and then started lighting all the candles in the room one by one. As all the candles in the room lit, Mayank switched off the light of the room. The entire room was lit with candles as if flowers of light bloomed in the gardens of darkness. The light of the candles was hitting Kaamna's earrings and creating shine. The shine of the earrings was driving Mayank crazy. Mayank lovingly tucked Kaamna's hair behind her ears and then made her sit in front of the cake. Kaamna cut the cake and as she was about to feed Mayank a piece, Mayank caught hold of Kaamna's hand which had a knife and while making eye contact with Kamna, he licked the cream with the knife. Kaamna's eyes lit up strangely and she started feeling shy after seeing Mayank. Mayank held Kaamna's waist and pulled her towards him and hugged her to his chest. Kaamna placed both her hands on Mayank's chest and got lost in his eyes. Mayank placed his right hand on Kaamna's cheek and started caressing her lips with his thumb. Kaamna closed her eyes, they both started kissing each other, Kaamna took her hands towards Mayank's head and then slowly started pulling his hair. The love of both of them started to blossom, both of them started burning in the fire of lust. Mayank took off Kamna's kurti and gave her a push. Kamna fell straight on the bed, Mayank turned Kamna and started kissing her neck, slowly moving to her back while kissing her and then slowly till her waist. Then suddenly Mayank turned Kaamna and opened the button and zip of her jeans. Kaamna also got so excited that she raised one of her legs and placed it directly on Mayank's chest and pushed him, Mayank fell on the bed and then Kaamna sat on his thighs and slowly opened the buttons Mayank's shirt one by one. Like a wild cat, Kaamna started scratching Mayank's chest. Mayank pulled Kaamna's hair and threw her on the bed. Both of them started extinguishing the fire of their bodies and gradually became completely engrossed in lust.

After both their desires were fulfilled, they both lay down on the bed in the same position. Mayank was writing many words with his fingers on Kaamna's bare back and Kaamna was guessing them.

You just wrote Kaamna , right? Kaamna asked.

No, I wrote kamini. Mayank said jokingly.

Yes, I am a and that too a big one. Kaamna replied laughingly.

And you are very sexy too. Mayank said.

I know. Kaamna said proudly.

Beautiful too. Mayank said again.

Everyone says this. Kaamna said while throwing tantrums.

For you, is there any difference between everyone and me or not? Mayank asked.

Oh idiot, If you were one of those people for me, you wouldn't be lying on this bed with me right now. Kaamna replied laughingly.

Then suddenly Kamna turned and started caressing Mayank by placing her hand on his cheek while looking lustfully into his eyes.

let's have another round. Kaamna said.

Yaar, you are so hungry for s*x! Mayank said.

Yes a lot, so satisfy my hunger right now. Kaamna said while spreading both her legs in front of Mayank.

Seeing Kaamna in this position, Mayank couldn't control himself and once again both of them jumped into the fire of lust.

Next day morning I was returning home from the ground after morning walk with Aman and Binay. Then we saw Mayank going to school on bicycle, he seemed a little disturbed.

Kya hero, how was yesterday, What did you give your girlfriend as a gift? Aman asked.

A smile appeared on Mayank's face after hearing Aman's words.

Looking at the smile on his face, it seems he also got some return gift. I said.

No, there is nothing like that. Mayank replied.

Then what are you thinking about so much? Aman asked.

Don't you guys know that Ravi ran away with Khushbu Bhabhi? Mayank said.

What nonsense are you saying! I asked.

I am not lying, As far as I know Khushbu Bhabhi has left a letter on which it is written that both of them love each other very much and want to spend their life together. Mayank replied.

Ok you go to school and concentrate on studies not on all these things. I said.

Mayank started towards school and we went towards Ravi's house.

See, till now in the society only the daughter used to bring bad name to her father by running away from home and now the daughter-in-law has also started running away and bringing bad name to her father-in-law. Binay said.

Shut up Binay, why do you always speak so negative? Aman asked.

I speak the truth not the negative. Binay replied.

Yaar, please both of you keep quiet. I said.

As soon as we reached near Ravi's house, seeing the condition there, it was certain that Ravi and Khushbu had run away. Everyone was talking about this incident. People were saying that the girl who did not step out of the house without anyone's permission, today took such a step. But I was sad that due to this action of Khushbu and Ravi, Karan's dream of teaching Khushbu remained unfulfilled. This action of both of them had confirmed that in this stage of adolescence, active hormones can make the teens do anything.

It was around 7:30 in the evening, I was sitting in front of my study table, I had my diary in my hand. This was the same diary in which Jenny's last letter to me was buried for many years. At that very moment Mayank came to me.

Vishal bhaiya, I need some help. Mayank said.

What? I asked.

Please make diagrams for my science practical. Mayank replied.

Ok, I will make it. I replied.

I was talking to Mayank when at that very moment I got a call from my father. As I picked up the phone, my father called me to the shop for a while. My shop was just 10 steps away from my house. I asked Mayank to wait for a while and walked towards the shop. As soon as I left, Mayank's eyes fell on my diary. As soon as he picked up my diary, Jenny's letter fell down from my diary. He picked up the letter and started reading...

"Dear Vishal, I know I have hurt you a lot but still you love me very much. Dear, today I am expressing my love to you, I am saying that I love you very much. I never understood how much you love me, I never appreciated your love and maybe I am being punished for these bad deeds. There are so many things in my heart that I want to tell you but it's too late now, So now I don't want to hurt you and myself anymore so I'm going far away from you forever. Please forgive me if you can. Your Jenny."

After reading the letter, Mayank placed the letter in the middle of the diary and put the diary back at the same place where it was kept.

And he left my house before I arrived. I don't know what was going on in Mayank's mind, he went straight to Aman's house and started knocking on the door. Aman's Bua(paternal aunt) opened the door.

Where is Aman Bhaiya? Mayank asked.

He is studying on the terrace. Bua replied.

Aman lived in his Bua's house. There was a small room on the terrace of the house. Aman used to study and sleep in the same room. Aman was studying when Mayank reached there.

Arey Mayank, what are you doing here at this time? Is there something? Aman asked.

What happened between Vishal Bhaiya and Jenny? Mayank asked the question directly without saying anything.

Have you gone mad that you have come to me just to ask this question and that too at this time? Aman asked.

I haven't gone mad, but I'll definitely go mad if you don't tell me what happened. I am beginning to fear that what happened to Vishal

Bhaiya might happen to me. Mayank said with the great emotion.

What happened to you Mayank, why are you talking like this? Aman asked.

I have read Jenny's letter, why did she separate herself from Vishal Bhaiya? Mayank asked.

Hearing Mayank's words, Aman got a shock, He widened his eyes and looked at Mayank angrily. Frustrated with Mayank's ignorance and questions, Aman came out of the room and sat on the cot laid in front of room. Both remained silent for a while, after a while Aman took a deep breath, raised his head and started looking towards the sky.

This open sky is so beautiful isn't it? Aman asked.

Yes. Mayank replied.

There are millions of stars in this sky, right? Aman asked again.

Yes, there are many. Mayank said looking towards the sky.

Choose one of these stars for yourself and close your eyes for a while. Aman said.

Mayank did exactly what Aman said. And got lost in a strange peace for a while.

Open your eyes and now tell me if you can see the star you chose earlier? Aman asked.

Yes, maybe this one..... no, maybe that one..... Aman Bhaiya, I don't understand anything, I can't identify my star. Mayank replied getting confused.

You are not able to identify your star because your star got lost in the crowd of millions of stars. Similarly, one of our own gets lost in the crowd of people of this world. Except for Polar star and constellations, all the stars in the sky are like the common people living in the world. Just as all the stars shine all night to create an identity for themselves, similarly every common people in this world struggles to create a unique identity for themselves. Some succeed some don't. But sometimes some people, in order to create their own identity, become part of a wrong group. And the same thing happened with Jenny. Aman explained to Mayank.

So had Jenny made friends with someone else? Mayank asked.

Jenny made friendship with a boy, his name was Rohan. Rohan used to do modeling and he also suggested to Jenny that she should also make her career in modeling because she is so beautiful. Jenny also started going to many fashion shows or events with him. Rohan started seducing Jenny. Jenny also started feeling that all this is a part of this profession, all these are common things in the fashion industry. And the closeness between them grew so much that they started having physical relations. Vishal was unaware of this, but he was completely devastated by Jenny's strange behavior. One day suddenly Roshni came with a letter from Jenny. Vishal was overjoyed after receiving Jenny's letter. Vishal started reading the letter and within no time Vishal's happiness got lost in the darkness of pain, his eyes filled with tears. Vishal was completely terrified and asked Roshni to make him talk to Jenny once under any circumstances. Roshni also went to school the next day with full hope that today she would talk to Jenny about this. When Roshni came home from school, Vishal was eagerly waiting for Roshni sitting on the doorstep of his house. Roshni had tears in her eyes. When Vishal asked, she said that forget Jenny... she has left this world. Roshni also came to know about this news after going to school, actually the day Jenny gave the letter to Roshni, it was the same night that she committed suicide by eating posion. Roshni told the whole incident to Vishal. Hearing Roshni's words, the ground slipped beneath Vishal's feet. Vishal sat there and started crying bitterly. Seeing this condition of Vishal, even Roshni could not stop herself and started crying holding Vishal's hand. The whole family got scared seeing both brother and sister crying together, then that day Vishal's family came to know about Vishal's love story. Aman said emotionally.

But why is Vishal Bhaiya getting punished for Jenny's deeds? If she also loved Vishal Bhaiya then why did she commit suicide? Maya asked emotionally.

Vishal was also worried about the same thing and started thinking that it was because of him that Jenny committed suicide. Giving the 12th exam 18 days after Jenny's death was no less than a battle for Vishal. Four months have passed since this incident, our 12th result has also been declared, Vishal has got a very bad result, Vishal and I had gone to R.S.P College for admission. Then we found Rosy Didi there, she was Jenny's cousin. She said that she was trying to meet Vishal for the last four months but was not able to meet him. She wanted to tell Vishal something about Jenny, then we sat in the shade of a tree. Rosie Didi started telling..." One day Jenny came to me, she was very disturbed and scared. When I asked her what was the matter, Jenny started crying. I wiped away her tears, made her sit next to me and held her hand and asked, then she fearfully told me that she had a physical relationship with Rohan. And like every time, Rohan took her to a room in the hotel but that day there were four other boys in the room. Rohan told Jenny that today she would have to entertain these boys. Jenny didn't like this and tried to leave. But before Jenny could leave from there, Rohan had closed the door of the room. Jenny requested Rohan to let her go and Rohan did not listen to a single word. By then a boy pulled Jenny's hair and threw her on the bed. Jenny started screaming in fear and asking Rohan for help but Rohan was standing and laughing. Then someone closed Jenny's mouth and someone held Jenny's hands and legs. After that someone took off all Jenny's clothes one by one and forcibly made physical relation with her. And Rohan was recording all this in the camera. After that Jenny started crying again and said that now those boys are doing wrong to her by blackmailing her. I have became a s*x slave of those boys, those boys scratch my body whenever they want, wherever they want, sometimes they hit me with belts, sometimes they slap me, sometimes they do such dirty things with me that I vomit.

I started feeling disgusted with myself, please save me from this quagmire, Rosy Didi. My heart trembled as soon as I heard Jenny's words. My mind became numb just thinking about all this happening to Jenny at such a young age. I was not able to understand what to do. Still I gathered courage and wiped her tears, hugged her and made her feel that I am with her and promised that I would definitely get her out of this quagmire. Three days after that she committed suicide. If I had known that she was going to take such a step, I would have told about it at home first and taken a strong action, But now I am helpless, neither is Jenny alive nor do I have any proof, I have only come to know that after Jenny's suicide, Rohan has fled to another city on the pretext of modeling. Look Vishal, Jenny also wanted to tell you all these things but she was afraid that after knowing the truth you might get angry with her and leave her. That's why I have a request to you, never keep hatred for Jenny in your heart..." Vishal became completely calm after listening to Roshni Didi, he had only tears in his eyes and nothing else. Aman said about the entire incident with tears in his eyes.

This world has become so bad that to satisfy one's lust one sacrifices someone else's love. Mayank said while wiping his tears.

***

It was evening time. Mayank was waiting for Kaamna outside the Youth Science Classes. The evening class was over, all the students were coming out of the class but Mayank did not see Kaamna.

Are you waiting for Kaamna, today you won't even be able to see her. Sakshi said.

Sakshi was Kaamna's batchmate and knew Mayank very well. Sakshi's father was a very good friend of Mayank's father. After Sakshi's father passed away, Mayank's father helped Sakshi's family a lot. This is why Sakshi considered Mayank like her brother.

Look, Sakshi, I am telling you first, today again don't say anything wrong about Kaamna. Mayank replied.

I will say it not once but a thousand times, why don't you understand that she is not a good girl. Sakshi said.

I have told you before that what you say doesn't matter to me and never will. Mayank replied.

Look Mayank, I don't want to argue with you, I just want to tell you that before the class starts, Kaamna has gone somewhere on a bike with a boy. Sakshi said.

He may be Kaamna's friend, maybe they both have some work, it's not a big deal. Mayank replied.

Mayank, I feel sorry for you, you are trusting Kaamna blindly, one day that trust will definitely break. Sakshi replied.

Sakshi started leaving from there, she too had gone some distance when suddenly Mayank called and stopped her. There was a strange turmoil in Mayank's mind that he could not understand. After knowing about the incident that happened with Jenny, even more strange thoughts started coming in Mayank's mind and he had lost control over his own thoughts.

After all, what do you know about Kaamna? Mayank asked doubtfully.

I wish I could tell you Mayank, but for now you just please understand that Kaamna is not the right girl for you. Sakshi replied.

Don't tell me who is right and who is wrong for me, I know Kaamna loves me very much. Mayank said.

I know you love Kaamna very much but you should know one thing, Kaamna loves only herself. Sakshi replied.

Look Sakshi, I am already very disturbed, if you want to say something about Kaamna then say it openly, don't make things like this. Mayank said.

Okay, if you want to know the truth about Kaamna then meet me at this same place tomorrow evening at same time. Sakshi said.

Really Sakshi, you are a big dramatist and a liar. If you have to tell the truth then tell it right now. Mayank replied.

Mayank you have forced me...Now I will tell you the truth about Kaamna. Come along with me. Sakshi said angrily.

Where? Mayank asked.

Digwadih no.-12, Officer Colony. Sakshi replied.

This is Kaamna's address. But why we are going there? Mayank asked.

To know the truth. Sakshi replied.

Mayank was not able to understand anything but still he sat in an auto with Sakshi and went straight to Digwadih no.-12, Officer Colony. Sitting on a bench in a small park in front of the main gate of the colony, Sakshi made a call one of her friend.

I'm outside your colony, I need a little help from you, come and meet me right now. Sakshi said to her friend on mobile.

After some time, a boy came there, he was wearing thick lens spectacles. he looked very simple and nerdy, as if someone scolded him in a loud voice, he would immediately cry.

He is my friend Harsh and he will tell you the whole truth about Kaamna. Sakshi said while introducing Harsh.

Hearing Sakshi's words, Mayank looked towards Harsh and started laughing loudly. Seeing Mayank laughing, Sakchi understood that Mayank was laughing seeing Harsh's look.

Don't laugh, he is Kaamna's ex-boyfriend. Sakshi said.

Just by looking at him it clear why Kaamna left him Mayank said while making fun of Harsh.

You are Mayank, right? Sakshi told me about you, At this time, you are crazy in love with Kaamna, that is why you are not able to understand anything, the day Kaamna will suck you like sugarcane and throw you away, you will understand everything. Harsh said.

What do you want to say? Mayank asked.

It's just that Kaamna is not a good girl. Harsh replied.

Even Sakshi say this but tell me what you want to say. Mayank said.

As soon as Mayank said this, Harsh immediately took out his mobile, played a video and gave it to Mayank. As soon as Mayank saw the video, he lost his senses, his eyes filled with tears and he screen off the mobile even before watching the complete video. This was Kaamna's private video with another boy.

I was in the same situation as you at this time. I know this is hard for you to accept right now, but no matter how much you try to deny it, this is the truth. Harsh said.

Mayank couldn't believe this and started trying to deny it. He was not ready to accept that Kaamna could do something like this. Mayank started thinking that what had happened to Jenny could now happen to Kaamna too.

Maybe that boy is blackmailing Kaamna and getting her to do all this. Mayank said.

Really Mayank, you are completely blinded by Kaamna's love. Didn't you see in this video that Kaamna is doing all the things as per her own wish. Harsh replied.

How can you say that Kaamna is doing all this of her own free wish? Mayank asked.

Look Mayank, now only time can answer this question to you because I can only give you answers, I can't break your illusion. Harsh replied.

Mayank couldn't sleep the whole night because of Kaamna's video. He waited the whole night for morning to come so he could go and talk to Kaamna. As soon as the morning came, Mayank stood outside the main gate of the school and started waiting for Kaamna. One by one all the students were arriving at school, after some time Kaamna's car came and stopped near the school gate. As soon as Kaamna got down from the car, Mayank called her.

Hi Mayank...Yaar, sorry I couldn't meet you yesterday. Kaamna said.

I need to talk to you about something. Mayank said.

Yes, tell me what to talk about. Kaamna said.

I met Harsh yesterday. Mayank said.

Oh that Champoo, who lives in my colony? Kaamna asked.

Yes, he showed me a video. Mayank said hesitantly.

After all that Champoo opened his mouth in front of you. Kaamna said.

Just say this once, all these things are lies, perhaps you had some compulsion behind this. Mayank asked with last hope.

Look Mayank, I really like you but it doesn't mean that we will be together in the future. I want to live my life fully enjoying and you are being too possessive about me. Kaamna replied.

Please Kaamna don't say that, I will always keep you happy. Mayank said pleadingly.

You keep me happy but on the bed. You really have great stamina. Any girl would want a guy like you in her bed. But this does not mean that you can fulfill every dream of that girl. Kaamna replied.

But I can do anything for you. Mayank said.

How will someone who himself travel in the general compartment of the train buy a plane's ticket for me? Kaamna asked irritably.

Next month I have a trial for the state cricket team and I am confident that I will get selected. Maybe after that I will play at the national level also. When I become a successful cricketer, I will definitely fulfill all your needs. Mayank said.

I know there is a lot of money in cricket, but it is not confirmed whether you will play national or not. And I don't want to spend my whole life with buffaloes in your stable. Kaamna said while insulting Mayank.

Mayank sat down on his knees in front of Kaamna and started crying and pleading.

Please Kaamna don't do this to me... I love you very much and will work very hard for you. Mayank said pleadingly.

You must work hard but for yourself, And the day you become a successful cricketer then

think about your future with me. Kaamna
replied.

Please Kamna don't do this to me I will die
without you. Mayank said cryingly.

Look, don't talk nonsense in front of me, If you
want... we can continue our relationship and
enjoy our life, but right now don't think about
the future. Kaamna said directly.

At that very moment the assembly bell rang,
Kaamna went straight inside the school and
Mayank kept sitting there and crying.

It was Sunday and we had a cricket match with
the neighboring team. Actually our ground was
situated between two localities. And often the
boys from other localities come early in the
morning to prepare for the police and BSF
physical exams and for morning walk. We all
became very good friends and hence to
maintain a positive competition among
ourselves, we used to play cricket matches
often. And the beauty of this match was that
senior and junior played together. There are
some seniors who were doing job, some people
were still preparing for services and some was
students. Often this match was held on Sunday
or any holiday and the losing team had to be
given a treat.

Aman Bhaiya, Mayank has not come yet.
Avinav said.

Look, do one thing, replace Mayank with an
extra fielder and send someone to Mayank's
house and call him. I said.

Avinav do this so that you go to call Mayank, I
will put an extra fielder in your place also.
Aman said.

Aman set all the fielders and the match started,
I was fielding on the leg side, right next to the
main gate of the ground. Four balls had been
bowled in the first over in which only three
runs had been scored. Aman bowled a brilliant
bouncer on the fifth ball. As soon as the
batsman hit the ball flying in the air, it was
coming right towards me. All the people of my
team were looking at me with a hope that I
might catch it. Then suddenly a voice came
from behind.

Vishal Bhaiya...Vishal Bhaiya.....Mayank hanged
himself... Avinav came running and said
cryingly.

As soon as I heard Avinav's words, I turned
back and ran straight towards Mayank's house.
The ball coming flying in the air as soon as it
hit the ground, it took a bounce and went out
of the boundary. Leaving aside bat, wickets

and incomplete match, everyone ran towards Mayank's house. As soon as I reached Mayank's house, I saw Mayank's mother crying while hugging her son's body. Mayank's father is crying while beating his head. Mayank's face had turned blue and his tongue had come out a little. His fists were clenched and his hands were completely stiff. Looking at his closed fists, it seemed that he had clenched his fists to prevent himself from trying to save himself. Perhaps Mayank was completely determined that he would leave this world. But he didn't think what would happen to his parents after that.

In this world people are born and die, it doesn't matter to anyone except those who are their own. Or those who consider them their own. Today Sakshi was also crying, not Kaamna because Sakshi considered Mayank as her brother and for Kaamna he was just a means to quench her lust. Kaamna will get another boy but Mayank's parents will not get their son and Sakshi will not get a friend like a brother again.

Like a raging volcano, these active hormones keep boiling every moment. Just as a volcano explodes due to internal pressure and the lava inside it comes out and destroys everything. Similarly, when the extreme emotions inside a teenager come out, they take the form of disappointment and frustration. Sometimes other people become victims of this frustration and sometimes it is themselves. Sometimes I feel that these active hormones are just like nuclear, if used in the right way it can bring light to someone's life and if used in the wrong way it can bring destruction in someone's life. The matter of concern is that the use of these nuclear is largely in the hands of knowledgeable people and scientists, but the use of active hormones is not in anyone's control.

***

An army of candidates gathered outside T.N.B Inter College, Bhagalpur. As if half the population of entire Bihar is present here. And this was certain to happen, after all today was the BPSC Prelims exam. A Bihari has the same relationship with civil services as a Chinese has with chopsticks. Even if they have to eat rice, they will eat it with chopsticks only. In the same way, a Bihari whether he is from Hindi medium or English medium, whether they are the child of a rich father or the child of a laborer or farmer, someone's wife or someone's daughter or someone working as a laborer himself, they will definitely give the civil services exam. There was one face of mine among these thousands of candidates. The entry had started, so I switched off my mobile and deposited it in a shop outside of the college and took entry inside the centre. When I came out of the center after giving the exam and took the mobile back, I saw that there were 12 missed calls from Aman. Then I made a call Aman.

Hello...Aman. I asked.

Yaar... Avinav had an accident. Aman said.

When and how? I asked.

This morning Avinav left the ground and went to the main road to learn bike and that too without a helmet. Then he met with an accident with a truck. Those who saw the accident said that it was the boy's fault and he was driving too fast. Aman replied.

Is he seriously injured? I asked.

He is badly injured, his head and face are injured. We all have taken him to P.M.C.H Hospital. Aman replied.

Only tow months had passed since Mayank's incident and yet another accident happened. I was not able to understand anything, only one thing was going on in my mind that I should reach Dhanbad as soon as possible. But before I could reach Dhanbad again a bad news reached me. I came to know that Avinav has been referred to Tata Main Hospital, Jamshedpur.

Binay and I were sitting with Aman in his room. Aman was very worried about Avinav. Aman always used to say that seeing Avinav reminds him of his younger brother who was kidnapped by naxalites in his childhood. From that very day, Aman's father became very scared and sent Aman to his Bua's house in Dhanbad to study. And that day Aman took a vow that he would eliminate naxalites from every corner of Bihar. Aman had already lost his brother but now he did not want to lose Avinav.

Don't worry everything will be okay. Binay said.

How can i not worry, it has been 46 hours since Avinav's operation but Avinav has not regained consciousness yet. Aman replied.

But what can we do, some things are not in our hands. Binay said.

My disquiet is increasing. Yaar, I want to see Avinav once. Aman said.

Then what are you thinking? Let's go. I said.

The same day, there was a train at around 2:15, all three of us boarded the same train.

We reached the hospital at around 8:10. Coincidentally we met Avinav's uncle just outside the main gate of the hospital. He told that Avinav has gone into a complete coma and there is no guarantee as to when he will recover. All three of us were shocked to hear this news. Aman's condition started deteriorating. Aman still controlled himself and went inside Avinav's room with us. The scene inside the room shuddered all three of us to the core. Avinav was lying straight on the bed without any movement. All the hair on Avinav's head was saved, and he was stitched and bandaged from head to jaw. His eyes were continuously looking at the ceiling of the room without blinking. For a moment I thought that maybe now Avinav will blink for his moment. But nothing like that happened. Due to his broken jaw, saliva was continuously falling from his mouth. Avinav's mother, sitting next to him, was sometimes wiping Avinav's saliva with her lap and sometimes her tears. Avinav's father was sitting holding Avinav's hand with tears in his eyes. It was very difficult to imagine what his parents were going through. Avinav's parents had one hope left that Avinav was breathing. But his breath was stuck between life and death. Avinav had become just a living corpse. Seeing all these things, Aman's steps automatically started moving backwards. Aman came out and started crying bitterly.

All three of us were sitting at Dhanbad station waiting for the train. For the first time in our lives we were all sitting together but there was no conversation between us. The reason for this was that Aman was leaving us all and going to village forever. All three of us were completely silent, perhaps all three of us were trying to suppress our emotions. Just when the train was announced, the emotions within us started becoming more intense. Then suddenly Binay got up and grabbed Aman's collar and pulled him towards himself.

Saala Kameena...you're leaving us all and running away. Binay said with tears in his eyes.

I placed my hand on Binay's shoulder and pulled him back.

Let him go. I said.

Then suddenly Aman hugged both of us tightly and started crying.

My father broke his backbone while teaching me. And what am I doing here, nothing...just preparation. It is better that I go to village and help my father. I will work in the farm during the day and study at night. Yes, there are very few resources in the village but there is definitely peace. Now I am feeling suffocated here. I'm tired of the noise here. Of course, after I leave, abuse me behind my back. But let me go now. Aman said flowing in emotions.

All three of us hugged each other and kept crying until the train arrived on the platform. As soon as the train arrived, Aman kept his luggage in the train and stood at the door of the train. The train gave the signal for the last time and started leaving the platform. As Aman was moving away from my eyes, the memories of our childhood were becoming fresh. Stealing gauva together from the garden, Taking bath in the pond together, Sometimes flying kites on the terrace with Aman, Sometimes eat together from the same plate, Sometimes laugh together sometimes cry together. We both kept looking at each other until we both disappeared from each other's sight. Only memories were left with me, my childhood friend was gone.

I came home and sat on my bed. Suddenly my eyes filled with tears. Then my mother saw me and I started crying as soon as I saw her. My mother knew what was going on in me. My mother put her hand on my head and sat next to me. Mother said that the one who gives pain also gives relief...Don't let your faith weaken, be patient everything will be alright. I placed my head on my mother's lap and closed my eyes. My mother placed her hand on my head and started caressing it. There was a special peace in mother's lap, there was no pain, no sorrow, and no worries about the future.

***

It is said that everything changes with time. Eight years have passed since the old days. A lot has changed today but one thing that has not changed is my destiny. This time too, even after crossing the threshold of the interview and coming back, my BPSC was not cleared. In our Bihar, when a child prepares for something, his entire family prepares along with him. With the hope that if a child becomes something after studying, then the future of many generations to come will change. I was sad that I was not able to live up to the expectations of my family. But there is happiness that perhaps after the establishment of Ram temple, a Ram Rajya would begin in India. I am happy that Shiksha also had a small but important contribution behind India's great success like Chandrayaan-3. Ultimately, Shiksha made her mother proud by clearing the ISRO Services exam. Shiksha is the first girl not only from her locality but from the entire district who is serving in ISRO. I am happy that now Phulwa Chachi doesn't have to sit on the ground in front of anyone's door. People started respecting her now. I am happy that although my two friends are not with me, they are living their dream lives wherever they are.

Binay finally cleared Group D exam. He is currently serving in South Eastern Railway, Chennai. And finally Aman also got the uniform of his dreams. Aman also cleared Bihar SI exam. Presently Aman is taking training as Sub Inspector from Bihar Police Academy, Bhagalpur. I am very happy that they all have progressed a lot in their life. But I am afraid of whether he will ever turn to look at me or not. It is natural to be afraid when you are left far behind your loved ones in life. Only after being a lone kite in the open sky, something else... No fear of getting cut and no hassle of fighting with anyone... But sometimes being alone doesn't make you feel like a king. It pushes you into the abyss of loneliness. And I too have become a victim of this loneliness........... I was sitting at my study table reflecting my life when my mother called me.

Look Vishal... who has come... Maa said.

I went and saw a tall and broad young boy standing at the door, he was Kabir. As soon as he saw me he hugged me.

You have changed completely Kabir..... I said.

Yes, but you haven't changed Vishal Bhaiya, you still seem to be of the same simple nature. Kabir replied.

Maybe that's why I'm left far behind in life. I said.

Don't say that... you were neither behind in the past nor behind today, you are just not able to recognize yourself. Kabir replied.

You have really grown up and started talking like a grown up. I said.

You were the one who used to say recognize yourself. Kabir replied.

Ok leave it..... and tell me how you remembered me after so many years. I said.

I remember you all the time but It took me so much time to prepare myself, nor did I have your contact number to talk to you. Kabir replied.

So you just came here to get my contact number. I asked jokingly.

No Vishal Bhaiya, I wanted to meet you and also tell you some good news. Kabir said smilingly.

What.....?

I have cleared the CDS exam. I am undergoing training at Officer Training Academy, Gaya from next month. Kabir said.

There was no limit to my happiness after hearing this. I placed one hand above my head and saluted Kabir.

Salute to lieutenant Kabir Ansari. I said happily.

Kabir laughed after seeing this action of mine. Suddenly his eyes filled with tears while laughing.

Shoorveers never cry....... I said.

But a person can cry....... Kabir said with tears in his eyes.

Looking at Kabir, I could not believe that he was the same boy whom I had last seen crying bitterly. Who was completely broken. And now the same boy is sitting in front of me with a different personality. It was true that after Kabir came back, my confidence had returned and all the loneliness had gone away.

Today one thing is being realized that understanding these active hormones is not as easy as we think. Sometimes these active hormones are as delicate as water bubbles. They are so delicate that they burst as soon as they are touched. And sometimes these active hormones are harder then diamonds. They are so hard that the more the circumstances rub them, the more they shine...

Fall like water.
Flow like water.
And
Be like water, not precious but equal and
important to everyone…